BONES

and the CUPCAKE Mystery

A Viking Easy-to-Read

BY DAVID A. ADLER

ILLUSTRATED BY BARBARA JOHANSEN NEWMAN

VIKING

VIKING
Published by Penguin Group
Penguin Young Readers Group, 345 Hudson Street, New York, New York 10014, U.S.A.
Penguin Group (Canada), 10 Alcorn Avenue, Toronto, Ontario, Canada M4V 3B2
(a division of Pearson Penguin Canada Inc.)
Penguin Books Ltd, 80 Strand, London WC2R 0RL, England
Penguin Ireland, 25 St Stephen's Green, Dublin 2, Ireland (a division of Penguin Books Ltd)
Penguin Group (Australia), 250 Camberwell Road, Camberwell, Victoria 3124, Australia
(a division of Pearson Australia Group Pty Ltd)
Penguin Books India Pvt Ltd, 11 Community Centre, Panchsheel Park, New Delhi – 110 017, India
Penguin Group (NZ), Cnr Airborne and Rosedale Roads, Albany, Auckland, New Zealand
(a division of Pearson New Zealand Ltd)
Penguin Books (South Africa) (Pty) Ltd, 24 Sturdee Avenue,
Rosebank, Johannesburg 2196, South Africa

Penguin Books Ltd, Registered Offices: 80 Strand, London WC2R 0RL, England

First published in 2005 by Viking, a division of Penguin Young Readers Group

1 3 5 7 9 10 8 6 4 2

LIBRARY OF CONGRESS CATALOGING-IN-PUBLICATION DATA
Adler, David A.
Bones and the cupcake mystery / by David Adler ; illustrated by Barbara Johansen Newman.
p. cm. — (Bones ; #3)
Summary: Detective Jeffrey Bones finds he does not need fancy equipment to solve
the school-lunch mystery of Not-Me Amy's missing cupcake.
ISBN 0-670-05939-0 (hardcover)
[1. Cake—Fiction. 2. Schools—Fiction. 3. Mystery and detective stories.]
I. Newman, Barbara Johansen, ill. II. Title.
PZ7.A2615Boe 2005
[E]—dc22
2004004432

Manufactured in China
Set in Bookman

Reading level 2.2

- CONTENTS -

1. Not-Me Amy

"Good morning,"

I said to Mr. Green, the bus driver.

"Good morning, Detective Bones,"

Mr. Green said.

That's me.

I'm Jeffrey Bones.

I'm a detective.

I solve mysteries.

Once I even helped Mr. Green

find his big yellow bus.

"Sit with me!"

Not-Me Amy called.

I like Not-Me Amy,

so I sat with her.

"How are you?" she asked.

"Cold," I said.

"Not me," Not-Me Amy said.

"I'm hot."

She always says, "Not me!"

That's why she's called Not-Me Amy.

I looked at Not-Me Amy.

She had on a coat,

a hat, gloves, and a scarf.

"You're hot," I said,

"because you're dressed for winter,

and you're sitting in a heated bus."

Not-Me Amy took off her hat,

scarf, and gloves.

She opened her coat.

7

Then she opened her lunch bag

and took out her sandwich.

"You like American cheese

on white bread," she said.

"Yes, I do," I told her.

"Not me," Not-Me Amy said.

"I like this.

It's apple mint jelly

on whole wheat bread."

Yuck! I thought.

Not-Me Amy showed me

the rest of her lunch.

She took out kiwi slices,

grapefruit juice,

and a spinach noodle cupcake

with green icing.

Yuck! I thought again.

"Well," I said.

"Look what I brought."

I opened my detective bag.

"A code breaker, detective powder,

and a walkie-talkie," I said,

and took everything out.

"Jeffrey, Amy," Mr. Green called to us.

"Aren't you going to school?"

Mr. Green had stopped the bus

in front of the school.

All the other children

were already off the bus.

"Oh, my," Not-Me Amy said.

"Let's hurry."

We quickly put our things away

and hurried off the bus.

2. Apple Mint Jelly

"Good morning," Mr. Gale said.

He's our teacher. He's so nice.

Every day he lets me take one thing

from my detective bag

and keep it on my desk.

"What will it be today?"

Mr. Gale asked.

I looked in my bag.

"Detective powder," I said,

and took it out.

"I may need it."

I knew I would need my book,

so I took it out, too.

We read in class,

and Mr. Gale taught us math.

Math is about numbers.

Then he gave us homework.

Jane said, "I hate homework."

Someone said, "Not me.

I love homework."

And you know who that "someone" was?

It was Not-Me Amy.

At lunch I sat next to Not-Me Amy.

I took out my sandwich,

American cheese on white bread.

Not-Me Amy took out hers,

apple mint jelly on whole wheat bread.

Yuck! I thought.

She drank her grapefruit juice.

Yuck! I thought again.

She put on her gloves,

reached into her lunch bag,

and said, "Hey!

Who took my spinach noodle cupcake?"

3. The Paper Towel Clue

"No one would take your cupcake," Jane said. "We don't take things that don't belong to us."

Tom said, "We also don't eat spinach noodle cupcakes."

"This is a mystery," Jane said. Jane, Tom, and Not-Me Amy looked at me.

"I know you brought

the cupcake to school," I said.

"You showed it to me on the bus."

I opened my detective bag.

"It's not in there," Not-Me Amy said.

I knew that!

"Of course your cupcake

is not in here," I said.

"Detective powder is."

I sprinkled powder on the table.

I looked at it for clues.

Jane, Tom, and Not-Me Amy

looked, too.

"You're not solving a mystery,"

Tom said.

"You're making a mess."

Tom was right.

I was making a mess.

I went to the kitchen

to ask Mike for paper towels.

"Hi," he said to me.

Then he gave me a cup of carrots.

"They're good for your eyes," he told me.

"Thanks," I said.

I reached into the cup.

"Hey, look," I said, and laughed.

"My carrots have Bones in them."

Mike looked at me, but he didn't laugh.

"It's a joke," I told Mike.

"My name is Bones, and my hand

was in the cup of carrots."

"Oh," Mike said.

"You know," he told me,

"a carrot is a vegetable,

and vegetables don't have bones."

I knew that.

I told Mike about the mess on my table

and asked if I could have some paper towels.

"Sure," Mike said.

He reached for a roll of towels,

and it fell.

Even before the towels hit the floor

I thought, *That's it!*

I solved the mystery

of the missing cupcake.

4. This Is a Mystery

I hurried back to our table.

"Where did you put your lunch?"

I asked Not-Me Amy.

"Right here," she said.

She pointed to her lunch bag.

"No, where was it

while we were in class?"

"It was in the closet," she said,

"on the shelf above the coats."

I smiled and told her,

"The bag was open.

Your cupcake fell out."

Not-Me Amy ate

the kiwi slices.

Then she threw the bag away

and said, "Let's go."

"Not yet," I told her.

First I had to wipe up

the detective powder.

When I was done

I threw away the towels

and my empty lunch bag.

Then Not-Me Amy and I

walked back to class.

"Welcome back," Mr. Gale said.

I told him about the cupcake.

"This is a mystery," Mr. Gale said,

"the mystery of the missing cupcake.

Do you think you can solve it?"

"I already did," I said.

Mr. Gale and Not-Me Amy

followed me to the closet.

"There it is," I said,

and pointed to the floor of the closet.

"Where?" Not-Me Amy asked.

"Where?" Mr. Gale asked.

Where? I wondered.

Not-Me Amy's cupcake

was not on the closet floor.

"It's okay," Mr. Gale said.

"You can both have some of my dessert."

Mr. Gale gave us some raisins.

"No," I told Mr. Gale.

"It's not okay.

I must find that cupcake!

I'm a detective,

and detectives solve mysteries."

5. I Don't Need My Code Breaker!

I thought about the cupcake,

and I thought about my detective bag.

I wanted to use my code breaker

to help me solve this mystery,

but there was no code.

I wanted to use my walkie-talkie,

but who would I talk to?

Then I looked at Not-Me Amy.

She wanted to eat the raisins.

She wanted to,

but she was having real trouble,

because she was wearing gloves.

Gloves! I thought.

I don't need my code breaker

or my walkie-talkie!

"I just solved the mystery," I said.

I told Not-Me Amy,

"You weren't wearing gloves in class.

You put them on at lunch."

Not-Me Amy looked at her gloves.

Then she looked at me.

"Where did you get your gloves?"

I asked.

"My mother gave them to me," she said.

"Don't you keep your gloves

in the pocket of your coat?" I asked.

"Yes," she said.

"You didn't have your coat at lunch.

So where did you get your gloves?"

I didn't wait for Not-Me Amy

to answer my question.

I answered it.

"Your gloves were in your lunch bag."

Mr. Gale said, "That's a strange place

to keep gloves."

He was right. He usually is.

"On the bus this morning," I said,

"we hurried to put our things away.

"I think you put your gloves

in your lunch bag

and your cupcake in your coat pocket."

Not-Me Amy went to the closet.

She reached into the pocket of her coat

and there it was.

She found her

spinach noodle cupcake.

Not-Me Amy shared it

with me and Mr. Gale.

Guess what?

Her spinach noodle cupcake tasted great!

Not-Me Amy promised

to give me and Mr. Gale the recipe.

FROM THE KITCHEN OF: **Not-Me Amy**

RECIPE FOR : **Jeffrey Bones and Mr. Gale**

DIRECTIONS: **To make your own spinach noodle cupcakes, just add a cup of cooked spinach noodles to your regular cupcake recipe. Of course, only cook or bake with the permission and supervision of a responsible adult.**